Happy Birthday, Mum!

An Ivy and Mack story

T0337186

Written by Juliet Clare Bell
Illustrated by Gustavo Mazali
with Szépvölgyi Eszter

Collins

Who and what is in this story?
Listen and say

Mack

Banjo

Ivy

Download the audio at www.collins.co.uk/839735

Mum

Dad

Grandpa

Croc

Today is Mum's birthday.
Mack says, "Is it morning?"

4

Ivy says, "Yes! Let's go."

6

Ivy says, "Mum ... ?
What are you doing?"

Mum says, "It's my birthday!"

Ivy says, "We know. But *you* don't make your birthday breakfast."

Mack says, "... *We* make it!"

Sit with Croc, Mum.

Ivy says, "We are making a great birthday breakfast!"

Mum loves her birthday breakfast.

Happy birthday, Mum!

Mack says, "Open your presents,
Mum."

Mum opens her presents from Ivy and Mack. "Wow! Things for my bike. Let's go on a birthday bike ride."

Yes!

Mack and Ivy say, "Mum open your present from Dad."

Mum says, "Not now. Let's go!"

Mum puts her new bell and water bottle on her bike.

They ride their bikes to the park.
But then ...

Mum says, "Oh no! My bike!"
Ivy says, "Oh no! Your new bell!"
Mack says, "Is it in here?"

Mum is sad. "Now I haven't got a bike or a bell."

Dad says, "Don't worry, open your present from me, Kate."

Mum says, "A new bike! Thank you!"

Ivy says, "Here is a new present, Mum."

I love it, Ivy!

We can ride our bikes

I can help in the garden

I can make dinner

Grandpa and Banjo are here.
They've got a birthday cake for Mum.
Grandpa finds Mum's new bell.

I love my birthday!

Picture dictionary

Listen and repeat

bell

birthday

birthday cake

presents

water bottle

1 Look and order the story

2 Listen and say

Collins

Published by Collins
An imprint of HarperCollins*Publishers*
Westerhill Road
Bishopbriggs
Glasgow
G64 2QT

HarperCollins *Publishers*
Macken House,
39/40 Mayor Street Upper,
Dublin 1
D01 C9W8
Ireland

William Collins' dream of knowledge for all began with the publication of his first book in 1819.

A self-educated mill worker, he not only enriched millions of lives, but also founded a flourishing publishing house. Today, staying true to this spirit, Collins books are packed with inspiration, innovation and practical expertise. They place you at the centre of a world of possibility and give you exactly what you need to explore it.

10 9 8 7 6 5 4 3

ISBN 978-0-00-839735-7

Collins® and COBUILD® are registered trademarks of HarperCollins*Publishers* Limited

www.collins.co.uk/elt

British Library Cataloguing in Publication Data

A catalogue record for this publication is available from the British Library.

Author: Juliet Clare Bell
Illustrator: Gustavo Mazali (Beehive)
Copy illustrator: Szépvölgyi Eszter (Beehive)
Series editor: Rebecca Adlard
Publishing manager: Lisa Todd
Product managers: Jennifer Hall and Caroline Green
In-house editor: Alma Puts Keren
Project manager: Emily Hooton
Editor: Deborah Friedland
Proofreaders: Natalie Murray and Michael Lamb
Cover designer: Kevin Robbins
Typesetter: 2Hoots Publishing Services Ltd
Audio produced by id audio, London
Reading guide author: Julie Penn
Production controller: Rachel Weaver
Printed and bound by: Pureprint UK

MIX
Paper | Supporting responsible forestry
FSC
www.fsc.org
FSC™ C007454

This book contains FSC™ certified paper and other controlled sources to ensure responsible forest management.

For more information visit: www.harpercollins.co.uk/green

Download the audio for this book and a reading guide for parents and teachers at www.collins.co.uk/839735